GB MAR 5 1992

R00089 87167

SO-AZK-068

J De Angeli

De Angeli, Marguerite,
 1889-
Thee, Hannah! /

 c1989.

PALM BEACH COUNTY
LIBRARY SYSTEM
3650 SUMMIT BLVD
WEST PALM BEACH, FL 33406

© THE BAKER & TAYLOR CO.

Also by Marguerite de Angeli

THE DOOR IN THE WALL

THE LION IN THE BOX

MARGUERITE DE ANGELI'S BOOK
OF NURSERY AND MOTHER GOOSE RHYMES

YONIE WONDERNOSE

THEE, HANNAH!

Marguerite de Angeli

PALM BEACH COUNTY
LIBRARY SYSTEM
3650 SUMMIT BLVD
WEST PALM BEACH, FL 33406

DOUBLEDAY

New York / London / Toronto / Sydney / Auckland

Published by Doubleday, a division of
Bantam Doubleday Dell Publishing Group, Inc.
666 Fifth Avenue, New York, New York 10103

Doubleday and the portrayal of an anchor with a dolphin
are trademarks of Doubleday, a division of
Bantam Doubleday Dell Publishing Group, Inc.

To place a credit card order of $25.00 or more, call, toll-free, 1-800-223-6834,
Ext. 9479. In New York, please call 1-212-492-9479. Or send your order, plus
$2.00 for shipping and handling, to the following address: Doubleday Readers Service, Dept. FM, P.O. Box 5071, Des Plaines, IL 60017-5071. Prices and
availability are subject to change without notice. Please allow four to six
weeks for delivery.

Library of Congress Cataloging-in-Publication Data
De Angeli, Marguerite, 1889–1987
    Thee, Hannah! / by Marguerite de Angeli.
        p.   cm.
    Summary: Nine-year-old Hannah, a Quaker living in Philadelphia
just before the Civil War, longs to have some fashionable dresses
like other girls but comes to appreciate her heritage and its plain
dressing when her family saves the life of a runaway slave.
    ISBN 0-385-07525-1
    [1. Quakers—Fiction.   2. Clothing and dress—Fiction.
    3. Slavery—Fiction.   4. Philadelphia (Pa.)—Fiction.]   I. Title.
PZ7.D35Th   1989
[Fic]—dc19   88-38788   CIP   AC

TEXT AND ILLUSTRATIONS COPYRIGHT © 1940 BY MARGUERITE DE ANGELI
INTRODUCTION COPYRIGHT © 1989 BY HARRY E. DE ANGELI
ALL RIGHTS RESERVED
PRINTED IN THE UNITED STATES OF AMERICA
OCTOBER 1989

In Memory of
DEAR AUNT HANNAH

"Aunt" Hannah Severns was approaching ninety when she and Mama first became acquainted. As their friendship grew she told stories of her childhood, which became the basis for *Thee, Hannah!*

The Quakers in Philadelphia were a very strong link in the Underground Railway, and Aunt Hannah really was involved with the woman and her child as related in the book. As Mama said later, "She had a rich and wonderful life, and was a wonderful example of how to grow old gracefully." Their friendship continued for the rest of Aunt Hannah's life, and, I believe, enriched both lives.

Harry E. de Angeli
January 1989

THEE,
HANNAH!

"Nine o'clock, and all's well!
Nine o'clock of a rainy night!"

HANNAH stopped talking for a moment to listen to the night watch cry out the time. She heard the cry again going on down the block, "Nine o'clock," and went on talking.

1

"This bonnet with the flowers and the pink ribbon will do, thank thee, I mean thank *you,*" said Hannah. "And does thee have—I mean—*have you* red satin for a dress?" Hannah was pointing toward the shelves of rich material that she saw in her mind. Sally was beside her, and though she, too, could see in her mind the shelves of material, she couldn't see Hannah's elegantly curved finger because the light was out. The two little girls were tucked into bed for the night. They were supposed to be asleep, but every night they played a game. They made believe they were fashionable ladies and were shopping.

"Hannah-Nanny, thee always chooses a red dress!" said Sally. "This time let *me* have the red dress!"

"Thee can have red, too, if thee likes!" said Hannah. "I guess I like blue better anyway." Then, making her voice sound as grown up and elegant as she could, she said, "I shall have the blue instead. Blue silk, thee knows, that rustles. I mean *you* know."

"And that bee-u-tiful parasol! My deah, I simply must have that!" said Sally. "Did thee, I mean *you,* say it is five dollars? I'll take it!" Hannah could see a faint shadow of Sally's hand as she pointed out the imaginary lace parasol.

Just then a voice came up the stairwell.

"Thee, Hannah, thee, Sally, are you still talking?" The little girls held their breath and made no answer.

"No more talking! Do you hear?" It was Gammy Welsh. "I'm going home now," she said. "Your mother has a headache, so be good quiet girls and go to sleep."

Nanny and Sally giggled under the quilt, but they stopped talking, and then Hannah yawned and turned over. She heard the town crier again but his call was far away. Sally yawned and turned over. They went to sleep.

Gammy Welsh lived across the street but came over each day to help take care of the big family on Twelfth Street. Then there was Mary Sullivan, the cook, and Norah, the waitress and upstairs girl, both of them from Ireland. But there were so many to care for and so much work in the four-story house that each child had to do his share. Sally and Hannah, who were the youngest, must make their own bed and tidy their room before school.

It seemed to Hannah as if she and Sally had hardly stopped talking about the new dresses and bonnets when Gammy Welsh was back again and calling them to get up.

"Come, Hannah! Come, Sally! There is scrapple for breakfast, but you won't have time to eat it if you don't hurry!" Hannah was still rubbing her eyes as she tumbled out of bed,

and Sally was into her shift before she had stopped yawning. They heard Father go downstairs while they were making their bed.

"Nanny!" Sally scolded, "thee knows Mother says, 'always tuck the bottom sheet in at the top!' And look! Thee's left wrinkles all along the edge! Make it smooth now!" Sally was almost two years older than Hannah and somehow it always seemed easier for her to do everything right.

"Thee's got it all crooked too!" said Hannah. "Look how the seam goes off to one side!" Hannah gave a jerk to the sheet that pulled it out entirely.

"Now look what thee's done!" said Sally. But just then Sister Rebecca came by the door on her way downstairs.

"Girls! Girls! Stop your quarreling! Come, come! Hurry and finish your work." Sally and Nanny smoothed the counterpane over the quilts and followed her.

Mother was at the table when they reached the dining room, and John came clattering down the back stairs after Charlie. The quiet time at the table seemed *very* quiet after the boys' heavy boots and the scraping chairs. Mother gave a little sigh.

Then Father said, "Yesterday I saw a cardinal in the garden, but this morning it looks as much like winter as ever. I do believe it is snowing." Mother looked out of the window.

"Snow is lovely, but it makes things more difficult for the poor," she said.

"Yes," said Father, "especially for those poor blacks that are trying to find their way to Canada." Hannah knew that Father meant the escaped slaves from the South who were helped on their way by the Friends. Father had a great concern for the slaves and helped them to escape whenever he could.

"Nanny and Sally, be sure to wear your gum shoes!" he said as he rose to leave.

"Yes," said Mother, "and, Hannah dear, comb thy hair a little better when thee goes upstairs. The front is all right, but the back looks like a chrysanthemum!"

Hannah scowled but went reluctantly to comb her hair again. How she hated it! Sally's hair waved softly and stayed in place; Hannah's was fine and straight and mouse-colored. She hoped that someday it would turn black and hang in ringlets as Cecily's did. Cecily lived next door and was her best friend. Hannah got her bonnet and started down the stairs. She held her head high, her chin out, and made believe she was a fine lady again. In her mind the bonnet became the fancy beribboned one she had chosen last night, and her drab little dress of printed delaine became a bright blue one of rustling silk. Instead of hanging in straight gathers, it was held out by the latest style in hoops. And just thinking of its effect, Hannah held her head so high that she missed the last step and fell flat on her nose. John was getting his high beaver out of the hatbox in the hall, and Charlie was buttoning on his jacket. They howled with delight, but Sally ran to help her.

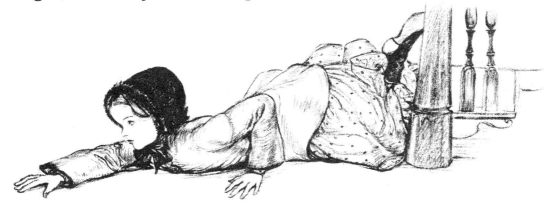

"Poor Nanny!" she said, and straightened her bonnet. Hannah stamped her foot.

"*Thee*, John!" Hannah said. "Oh! Thee little *you*, thee!" John laughed louder and went out the door. Rebecca came out to see that the girls got off safely. She smoothed Nanny's ruffled feelings and tied her bonnet.

The snow was spitting down in tight little bits. "The kind that stays," Mother had said. Instead of melting when it touched the brick pavement, it blew about in a misty powder.

Cecily came out of her house next door and called for the girls to wait. As always, she was daintily dressed, and the ribbons of her flower-trimmed bonnet just matched her blue eyes. Her hooped skirt swayed with the motion of her walk and showed the pantalettes below. Her dark curls peeped out of her bonnet beside the roses inside the brim.

To Hannah she was lovely. Besides, instead of going to plain Quaker Meeting as Hannah did, she went to Saint Peter's

where other fashionable people went. There they had music. Hannah had often heard it when she went to Aunt Phoebe's house on Pine Street. Cecily caught up with the girls.

"Hello! Hannah-Nanny," she said. "Hello! Sally-Alley!"

The boys were way ahead; John jumping over all the hitching posts, and Charlie with his head down against the wind and his nose in a book.

Hannah's everyday bonnet of velvet made a scoop for the wind and held her ears so tight she had to turn her head to hear what Cecily was saying. It was not stiff like her Go-to-Meeting one, and it had a soft little frill that framed her face, but how she wished it had flowers like Cecily's!

The boys turned off at Chestnut Street to go to their own school. Just as they reached the corner two bigger boys pounced on them as they often did and drummed with their fists on Charlie's hat. John managed to get out of the way, but Charlie's beaver was pushed down to his ears, and he was so angry he couldn't speak. Before he had worked his hat up where it belonged the big boys were well on their way in the other direction, calling as they went: "Quaker, Quaker! Mashed pertater!" Charlie was ready to throw his book at them, but just then the schoolmaster came around the corner.

"How is thee this morning?" he asked as he passed. Charlie swallowed his anger and ran to catch up with John, who was enjoying the fun because he had not been caught.

Hannah, watching, stamped her foot.

"I'd fix 'em!" she said. Sally pulled at her arm and said:

"Come along, Nanny. Thee knows that is Old Spotty talking to thee!"

"Old Spotty?" said Cecily. "Who's Old Spotty?"

"That's what Gammy Welsh calls Satan," said Sally. "She

says he whispers in our ears, and makes us do wrong and say what we shouldn't." Cecily laughed.

They went on to school through the wind-blown snow.

When recess came the snow was coming down in thick swirls. It lay two inches deep on the ground, and the girls stayed inside.

"If it keeps up like this," said Teacher Elizabeth, "we shall have to send you all home before school is over!" She stood looking out at the storm.

Hannah hoped it *would* keep up! Sure enough! The class had just finished reciting after recess when the headmistress came into the room and dismissed them for the day. By the time the girls had their things on and were ready to go the storm was growing steadily worse. They had to hold on to each other to keep from being blown back by the wind, and the thick veil of snowflakes made the rows of houses, the horsecars, and even the people look as if they were made of blue cardboard.

Twisting and turning, sometimes facing the wind and sometimes walking backward, they finally reached home.

Before the noon dinner was ready Father came home. He said the storm was getting worse and that horses were having a hard time to keep on their feet in the streets. Hannah ran to the parlor window to look out.

The snow was a thick smother, and the houses across the street looked faint and far away. She heard the oysterman calling.

"Oysta-oh, Oysta-oh!
Yere dey go, Oysta-oh!
Clams to bake, clams to stew,
Clams to make clam fritters too!"

THE SNOW was so thick Hannah could hardly see the man behind his cart. She called, "Gammy Welsh! Gammy Welsh!

Come quick! Here's the oysterman!" She ran out through the hall and met Gammy Welsh at the back stairs.

"We'd better get him now, while we can! Thee, Nanny! Tell him to come to the back door." Gammy Welsh hurried out to meet him.

In a few minutes Norah came to announce dinner. As they kept the silence at the table for a moment, the fire crackled in the fireplace and the snow made little hissing sounds against the window. When Father unfolded his crisp napkin, Hannah knew it was time to stop looking at her plate.

"Since you cannot go back to school," said Mother, "thee, Sally, and thee, Nanny, had better help Alice to whip the seams on your dresses."

"And thee, John, must clear the walk in front of the house, even though it is still snowing and will have to be done again. Charlie, I heard cook say the kindling was low. Thee split some after dinner." Charlie remembered then to tell how the boys had thumped on his hat. Norah was in the room, and she whispered in his ear:

"Do ye be comin' through the kitchen after dinner, and I'll tell ye how to fix 'em!" she said.

When dinner was over Rebecca and Alice and the two little girls went up to the sewing room, and when she had put away the loaf sugar in the sitting-room closet Mother joined them.

"With so many hands we should be able to finish those two dresses," said Mother, as she found needles and thimble for Sally and Hannah.

"But I don't *want* a thimble!" said Hannah. "I can push the needle through on the windowsill."

"Thee must have a thimble, Nanny. Thee must learn to do it right!" said Sally. "When I was nine I didn't like a thimble either, but now I do."

"Thee's not so *very* old now," said Hannah. She struggled to keep the thimble on her finger, but it kept falling off. She stamped her foot with impatience.

"Hannah, dear, don't allow thyself to lose thy temper!" Mother said.

The girls sewed quietly for a while. The snow was coming down faster than ever. Hannah stopped her sewing and went to the window to watch it.

It had piled up around the posts of the grape arbor; it loaded the branches of the peach and cherry trees. It ridged the brick wall at the back of the garden and heaped the corchorus bush on every branch. It seemed to Hannah a long time ago that she had sat in the apple tree and it had been too warm even to play.

The glass was cold, and a chilling draft came in at the sill. Just then they heard the front door and the vestibule door open and close. Then a dragging of feet, and Father breathing so heavily that Mother rushed out to see what was the matter. He had sunk down on the chair in the hall, too exhausted to speak.

"It is the worst in years!" he said. Hannah ran to the window in the parlor, but a coating of frost was forming so she could just peek out, then she came running back.

"There's someone out there leading a horse, and he fell! Hurry! Hurry! Gammy Welsh! Gammy Welsh!" But Gammy Welsh was already there. She had heard the excitement in the hall. She wrapped her shawl over her head and was nearly blown away by the blast of wind and snow that greeted her as she opened the outer door. The man who had fallen was on his feet again and was trying to tie the horse to the hitching post. He managed to get a blanket over him, then stumbled up the steps to the house. Gammy Welsh helped him in the door and into the hall, where he slipped again. By that time Father was feeling better and, with Mother and Gammy, helped get him into the back parlor and onto the sofa. Then they saw that he was a Friend, an elder who sometimes felt a "concern" to come to the Meeting in Philadelphia. At first he couldn't speak, but Gammy brought a hot drink, and soon he was able to sit up.

"But my horse!" was the first thing he said. "He will freeze!" He started to get up, but the two boys said they would attend to the horse.

Gammy Welsh set a match to the fire in the back parlor, and Joshua Haines told about his journey through the storm. "I had started before it began to snow and was well on my way before I realized that we were to have a bad storm," he said. "Then I knew that if I could reach thy home, thee would take me in."

"Of course we would!" said Father.

"Now," said Mother, "here we are all safe and warm out of the storm. How thankful we should be!"

"Yes," said Father, "but I can't help wondering how that poor black woman is faring. We sent her off in a wagon under cover of a load of groceries, but I'm afraid they weren't able to go on. A Friend was to take her as far as Buckingham today. From there she was to go with another Friend to New York, but this blizzard will disarrange their plans." Hannah listened while they talked of the poor Negroes who were held in slavery and what was to become of those who tried to escape and failed.

Norah came in to light the lamps and to tell them that supper was ready. As they sat down she brought a heaping plate of hot biscuits and put them down near Joshua Haines's place. He was busily talking but ate as if he were very hungry. John and Hannah couldn't help seeing how he liked Mary Sullivan's biscuits, and every time he took one John pinched Hannah. She began to count and could hardly keep from giggling when he reached for his tenth! He was talking all the while and, with a sweep of his arm, showing how well the corn had grown last summer in Jersey. His hand just grazed the edge of the water goblet and overturned it onto the white cloth. He didn't know what to say!

"Never mind, it is nothing!" Mother said, and sopped it up with her napkin. Hannah opened her mouth and her eyes as Friend Joshua reached for another biscuit!

The storm continued all night. But at daylight it stopped snowing, and the sun rose bright and clear. The snow drifted so high in places that a great mound of it came in when Father opened the front door. Then there were other places where the wind had swept the street bare. Father was late getting to his work, and there was no school.

Hannah and Sally played house with Old Heavy Head, the big doll, and their dishes until Mother and the older girls were ready for them to whip seams again. The big doll had her own chair and sat up to the table. Her real name was Sophronie.

"Thee knows, Nanny, *that* is not the way to drink tea from thy saucer!" said Sally. "And thee makes a noise just like Norah

21

does. Take it *so!*" Sally showed her how it should be done, without putting the finger the *least* bit into the saucer.

Then Father came home for dinner. He was full of tales about the damage done by the storm.

"Get together all the outgrown clothes you can find!" Father said. "We shall have to help those who are in need." Then he added, "I have a surprise for you, Nanny and Sally." He got up from the table, and Mother excused the girls from helping Norah clear away. Father came in from the vestibule with a sleigh! Not just an ordinary sleigh. It had beautiful curved runners and a handle at the back to push it, and the curved runners were ram's horns!

"These horns came into the chemical plant with the bones the other day, and one of the men helped me to make this." Hannah was filled with delight. Not even Cecily had so beautiful a sleigh! John and Charlie came running to see it and promised to give the girls a ride when they were ready. Hannah ran up the stairs after her bonnet and cloak so fast that she caught her foot in her dress and tore the front of it.

"Tch! Tch! Tch!" said Mother. "Now thee will have to wait till Rebecca can mend it! Haste makes waste, thee knows!" Yes! Hannah knew! It happened to her every day. She could hardly keep the angry tears back as she stood while Becky sewed her dress for her.

At last it was done. Sally waited for her in the doorway with her things.

The sleigh was a great success, and Hannah was so proud to show it to Cecily, who came out to try it.

"Pepper pot, all hot! all hot!
Makee back strong! makee live long!
Come buy my pepper pot!"
HANNAH listened to the pepper-pot woman. She hadn't been
along for days, not since before the big snow. When she heard

the cry she knew that it was almost suppertime. She turned from the long mirror between the windows.

"Quick!" she thought. "I must be quick, or Father will see me!" She whisked Mother's silk shawl off her head, ran to the parlor door to see if the coast was clear, then up the stairs to the highboy in the hall where she put the shawl in its place. She heard Sally coming down from the third-floor bedroom and pushed the drawer shut just in time.

"Thee looks like the town cat when he's eaten a bird! What's thee been doing?" Sally asked.

But just at that moment Father came in, and Hannah didn't have to answer. Both girls scrambled down the stairs to greet him, Hannah tumbling on the last step as usual.

"Thee chokes me!" He laughed as Hannah hugged him. "And it is too cold to stand here. Brrh! They tell me that the river is frozen from shore to shore, and they have cleared the snow enough so there is excellent skating!"

"There come the boys," said Mother as the back door banged. "They will want to go if there is skating."

"And so will we! So will we!" cried Hannah. She frisked around, holding Father's hand, and Sally echoed, "So will we! So will we!"

"Skating! Skating!" called John and Charlie, bursting into

the room. Mother held her head. Gammy Welsh came to the door.

"What's all this I hear about skating?" she asked. "You'd better get yourselves ready for supper. Thee, Hannah, see if thee can't get that bunch of hair smooth at the back. What has thee been doing? Thee looks like a scarecrow!" Hannah scampered out and up the stairs. Sally had smoothed her hair before she came down, but then she hadn't been playing "lady" with Mother's shawl.

There was a great deal of excited whispering in school the next day and a great deal of rattling of skates. Mother had said that Sally and Hannah might go skating with John and Charlie when school was over. Hannah could hardly wait for lessons to be over and kept looking out of the window to make sure that it hadn't begun to snow again.

At last it was time. Cecily's mother had said she might go too, if the boys would look after her. As the girls neared Chestnut Street they saw John and Charlie laughing and shouting and pointing at the big boys who liked to tease them and drum on their hats. The big boys didn't seem to think it was funny and were shaking their hands as if they hurt. John and Charlie joined their sisters and Cecily across the street.

"Oh!" said John, holding his sides. "What fun! I guess that's the last time they'll try that trick! Norah helped us to stick our hats full of tacks!"

The girls laughed, and Hannah said, "Old Spotty must talk to Norah sometimes too."

It was very exciting to be going toward the river instead of toward home after school. The snow was piled high on the sides of the walks and lay thick enough in the streets so that there was sleighing. Boys and girls, young men and young women, crowded the walks on their way to enjoy the ice. Skates clinked against their shoulders, and the crisp air was filled with their laughter.

When they reached the river, Sally, Hannah and Cecily sat on the edge of the wharf while the boys helped them on with their skates.

Boats that had been caught in the sudden cold were frozen at the wharf. Besides the skaters, horses and sleighs went up and down the frozen river, and vendors of every kind cried their wares. A woman sold pepper-pot from a wagon; the pretzel man pushed his cart over the ice; the muffin woman carried her basket on her head. A crowd of young people had even built a fire on the ice. There hadn't been a freeze like it for years!

"Hannah!" said John, "thee be careful how thee stays away from air holes!"

"I will!" said Hannah. "I will!" She wobbled and swayed a little to get her balance. Sally took her hand, and Cecily got to her feet.

"Wait now," called Charlie, "till we get our skates on!" Then off they all went, holding each other's hands. Hannah's ankles were not very strong, because she had only begun to skate the year before, but she felt free and happy to be gliding along as she sometimes did in a dream.

"See how well I can go alone!" cried Hannah, her arms outstretched to keep her balance. Then she struck a rough place in the ice and fell.

"Oh, Nanny!" said Sally. "*See* now! Is thee hurt?" She helped Hannah up, and they all joined hands again.

"Let's buy muffins!" said Cecily. "Has anybody any pennies?" She brought two out of her muff.

John had the money Father had given him "for emergency," he said. Charlie had a little from his allowance. Sally and Hannah had only a penny each. They bought muffins and munched them as they skated. No homemade muffins ever tasted half so good!

"See how much better I can do now," cried Hannah. She let go of John's hand and started off by herself, her unhooped skirt blown against her knees and showing her sturdy woolen stock-

ings. The girls watched while she sailed proudly along, but just as Charlie called out a warning a sleigh caught Hannah's heel and sent her flying across the glare of ice. Two or three children standing by went down, too, as she bumped into them, but, worst of all, Hannah stopped sliding right over an air hole and almost went into the river! It wasn't a large air hole, but she got her feet soaking wet.

"Oh, Hannah! I told thee to stay by us!" scolded John. "Now we'll have to go home, and you've spoiled all the fun!" Poor Hannah! She was wet and miserable enough! But she wouldn't let John see how badly she felt! She stamped her foot when she got her skates off, then burst into angry tears.

"Never mind, dear Nanny," Sally comforted. "Our mother will fix thee, and I don't mind going home, honest! Does thee, Cecily?" Cecily was disappointed, and John and Charlie scolded all the way up the hill where they went to get the omnibus. There wasn't enough money left for them all to ride, so John rode with Hannah, and the others walked.

Hannah was very cold, even with her feet in the straw that covered the floor of the omnibus. By the time the bus man let them out at Twelfth Street she was shivering. Gammy Welsh sent her right upstairs, where Mother helped her undress, wrapped her in a warm merino robe, and tucked her in.

"Now, Hannah dear, stay in my bed while Norah gets hot water. I will send her up to help thee."

How good Mother's bed felt! There was a special comfort in Mother's bed, Hannah thought. She wondered if it were because of the delicious smell of lavender in the sheets. But there was lavender in all of the bed linen! So it couldn't be that. She was almost asleep when Norah came up to help her bathe.

"Sure, and it's a wonder ye didn't drowned yerself!" said Norah, pouring the warm, soapy flood over Hannah's cold feet. " 'Tis the pneumony ye'll be after gettin' if ye don't look out!"

Hannah giggled. Then Gammy Welsh came up with a cup of ginger tea. Ugh! It nearly scalded Hannah's throat, but it did warm her!

"Thee, Hannah, gets *this* instead of the chocolate that Mary Sullivan's giving to the others!" said Gammy. "Thee knows if thee hadn't been so proud and gone off by thyself, it wouldn't have happened." Mother came in with dry clothes and shoes and helped Hannah comb her hair.

"I *wish* it was black and curly," said Hannah. "I *wish* I was

pretty like Cecily! I *wish* I could have a blue dress and wear pantalettes!"

"Why, *Nanny* dear!" Mother said. "Whatever in the world is the matter with thee? Thy father does everything he can to make thee happy! And thee is such a bright spirit most times! But sometimes thee lets Old Spotty talk to thee. Sometimes thee troubles me with thy naughtiness. Pretty *is* as pretty *does,* thee knows."

When she went down to supper Father said, "Why, thee's as sweet and fresh as a daisy!" Then Hannah was happy!

"Shad! Fresh Delaware shad! Fresh shad!
First of the season.
You buy any shad? You buy any catfish?
Shad! Shad! Fresh shad!"

HANNAH looked out of the doorway into the early morning. Norah was cleaning the white marble steps. Hannah skipped lightly down to the brick walk.

"Whin ye hear that cry," said Norah, "ye'll be knowin' that spring is almost here. It'll not be long now till it's time to turn out the house for the spring cleanin'." She finished wiping the steps and went in.

Hannah lingered a moment. Father didn't like her to be out on the street in front of the house except when she was on her way somewhere. "It's too public for little girls," he said. But it was so pleasant to be out before anyone was about, to see the woman selling fish and the hominy man who was coming around the corner.

March had blustered and rained its way through, but it was nearly over. The air was filled with the smell of moist earth and of growing things.

Hannah could see through the gate of the garden large patches of green where the snow had melted in the sun, and along the edge of the flower bed little swords of green showed where hyacinths would grow.

"Yes," thought Hannah, "and there will be flowers on Cecily's new bonnet, too, but mine will just be the same old *hot scoop!*" Sally called down from an upstairs window. The baker's wagon came rattling around the corner. The city was waking up. Hannah went in to breakfast.

"Hannah dear, thee must do thy stint early today. Thee, too, Sally," Mother said. "You are to go with Gammy Welsh to the bonnet maker's to be fitted this morning. While you are down there so near you can go to the Second Street Market." Hannah was delighted to hear that. It made up a little for having to be fitted for another stiff old bonnet. It was to be a straw bonnet, but it would be lined and just as hot as the winter one. Hannah couldn't see why Father insisted on making them wear the old things!

Sally didn't seem to care, and Rebecca and Alice at *least* had hoop skirts. Not big ones but *hoop* skirts! Like Cecily's. And the dress materials!

"Why can't we have bonnets and dresses like Cecily wears? *She's* a nice girl," Hannah begged. "Why must ours be dull and ugly?"

"Of *course* Cecily's a nice girl!" agreed Father. "But *thee's* a Friend! It would be out of place for thee to wear the frills and furbelows that some people wear. Let thy spirit shine through. Then thee's as handsome as anybody!" Hannah pouted. She didn't even know how to let the spirit shine through, and she didn't think it would make much difference anyway.

Father reached over to pat Hannah's hand. "And when thee's down at the Second Street Market get Gammy to take thee to Jakob Gratz's stall and bring home some pot cheese for me. *Thee* can get it!" And he counted out the money for Hannah to buy it herself!

By the time Hannah and Sally had done their stints on their samplers Gammy Welsh was ready to go. They ran to put away their work and get their things.

Hannah got her bonnet from its box.

"Hurry, Nanny!" said Sally. Hannah pinched her lips together and scowled at the offending bonnet. At the top of the stairs she dropped it, then, with a little kick, sent it flying! Sally looked horrified.

"Oh, Hannah!" she said. "What's thee done?" Hannah held her breath too. She knew how expensive bonnets were and how Mother made them take the best care of them. Worst of all, the bonnet went all the way downstairs, and just as it landed at the bottom Father came across the hall and stepped right on it! He picked it up and brushed it and shook his head sadly at Hannah, who came slowly to the foot of the stairs.

"Hannah, dear!" He sighed. "I thought thee was growing up. I thought thee had learned a little what thy bonnet stands for. I see thee hasn't." He went out the front door, but Gammy Welsh was right there.

"*Thee, Hannah!*" she scolded, "get thee out to the corchorus bush and shake Spotty off thee!" She put Hannah's bonnet on her and sent her out the side door. Hannah walked slowly down the brick path, her head bowed. She hadn't meant really to kick the bonnet down the stairs. She had meant to kick it only a

little. But she still couldn't see why she had to wear the ugly old thing. Spears of grass peeked up at her through the ground! Sparrows were pecking at the crumbs Norah had thrown out. The town cat was walking with dignity along the top of the brick wall. Hannah gave herself a little shake under the corchorus bush, and then she saw the yellow buds along the stems. They were full to bursting! What a lovely world it was! She ran back to Gammy Welsh and hugged her around the knees.

"I'm sorry, Gammy," she said. Gammy tied her bonnet strings, gave Hannah her little mitts, and they started off with Sally.

After the fitting at the bonnet maker's the trip to market was exciting. Gammy filled her large basket with meat and with vegetables—beets, cabbage, salsify, and carrots. Then Hannah bought the pot cheese for Father.

When they got home it was dinnertime.

"Cecily was here asking for thee, Nanny," said Mother. "I told her thee might come over after dinner."

Hannah left by the side door and slipped through the gate between the two houses. Cecily saw her from the window and ran to let her in.

"Hello! Hannah-Nanny!" she called. "Come upstairs to the sitting room. We can play with the dollhouse and dress up. Mamma says we may." They ran up the stairs. The sun shone through the lace curtains, and there was a fire in the grate. Cecily's mother was sitting by the fire with a book. "Good afternoon, Hannah dear!" she said. Hannah thought she was very pretty, with her lace collar and plaid silk dress, and lovely drop earrings that glittered when she moved.

Near the window stood Cecily's dollhouse. Hannah loved it. There were two floors, all finished just like a real house! There was horsehair on the chairs and a black mantel that looked like marble. There was a stove in the kitchen and a real copper teakettle besides all the tin cooking pots and a set of china dishes.

"Here's a dress for you," said Cecily, "and my sash that you can wear. It's my second best, so be careful."

"Oh!" said Hannah, "what a lovely sash! How I wish Father would let me have one!" She put on the dress, and Cecily tied the sash. Hannah peered at herself in the long glass that hung between the windows. The sash was bright pink and stood up in a stiff bow. Hannah sighed with delight. Cecily's mother went out of the room and left them to play.

Cecily put on the dress she was to wear, then she said:

"Now we will play house! I'll be the mamma that lives in the dollhouse, and you can be the lady that comes to call."

They played happily till Susie brought them a tea party. When they had eaten Hannah knew that she must go home. How she hated to take off the sash!

"You can borrow it if you want to," said Cecily. "You can try it on and make believe it is yours. I only wear it with my summer dresses anyway." She folded it up neatly, and Hannah tucked it down inside her dress. She had a "stop" in her mind that it was not quite right. Perhaps Spotty was talking to her again! But she *did* want to wear the sash! "No one will know I have it," she thought.

When Mother met Hannah at the foot of the stairs the sash seemed to burn a hole right through her dress, but Mother didn't notice anything and kept on down the hall, so Hannah then ran quickly up to the bedroom. She wiggled to get the sash out from under her dress, then went over to Rebecca and Alice's room to try it on. The mirror was larger there. She managed to tie the sash and twisted around to see how it looked. Just then she heard Gammy Welsh on the stairs.

Hannah listened to see if she were coming all the way to the third floor. She was! Off came the sash! Hannah stuffed it into the little drawer of the bureau. She pushed the lid off something —*something soft and smeary!* But she didn't dare to look. Gammy was coming into the room with an armful of laundry.

"What's thee doing *here?*" she asked. "Thee has a guilty look! Hannah, child, what's thee doing now?" But Hannah was brushing the back of her hair and didn't answer. Gammy put the clothes away. "I suppose thee likes to come in here and make believe thee's grown up," she said as she closed the bottom drawer of the bureau. "I used to like that too." She went downstairs, and Hannah breathed a sigh of relief. She opened the little drawer softly and took out the sash. It had a great smear of Alice's pomade on it! It was ruined! "That's what comes of letting Spotty talk to me, Gammy would say," she thought. *"Now* what will I do?" She stood thinking for a moment, then ran up to the fourth floor and back to the attic that opened off the hall. Right near the door stood a large bedding chest. Hannah opened it and thrust the spoiled sash deep down beside the quilts that were kept there.

"Now," she thought, "no one will see it till I can find what to

do. Cecily won't need it for a long time, and maybe *something* will happen before that."

She ran down the stairs to the third floor just as Sally came to call her to supper.

"Yere's de whiteywash man!
White whiteywash! Brown whiteywash!
Yellow whiteywash! Green whiteywash!
Wash! Wash! I'm about!"

HANNAH called out the window, "Whiteywash man, whiteywash man!" She had been sitting there waiting for him to come along. It was getting warmer every day, and the windows were open. At breakfast Mother had said:

"Hannah, please take thy work and sit by the window where thee can see the whitewash man and call to him as he goes up the alley. He's sure to be along today, and we need to have the cellarway whitewashed. We want it fresh and clean to store food for Yearly Meeting Week. So don't miss him!"

"Has thee heard from the Friends at Horsham then?" asked Father. "Are they all coming for Yearly Meeting?"

"No," said Mother, "the William Rhoads family cannot come. Nancy has been ill, and Margaret says she is afraid to attempt it. So I am asking John and Mary Evans and the girls in their place. They usually go to Grandmother Evans, as thee knows, but this year she is not able to have them."

After the whitewash man had finished Hannah found Sally in the kitchen, cleaning the silver tea set and talking to Mary Sullivan. Gammy was getting ready to make fruitcakes and cookies.

"Thee, Hannah," she said, "had better get thy father's stocks ironed, then thee can help me to seed and cut up raisins and pick meats from the black walnuts." Hannah got out the heavy ironing board and tested the irons. She loved to iron the fine linen stocks. Father said she did it better than anybody. Norah always stretched the bias edge, and Sally sometimes scorched them. Father sputtered if they were not done just *so*.

When she had finished Gammy said:

"Now thee can fix the raisins and the nuts. Mind thee gets no shells among them, and get all the seeds out of the raisins!" Hannah loved to watch Gammy Welsh when she baked, and she thought over and over what fun it was.

First Day dawned clear, warm, and beautiful. It seemed as if spring had really come to stay. Forsythia and Corchorus blossoms were out, and hyacinths, daffodils, and narcissus made the air fragrant.

All of the girls and the two boys, followed by Mother and Father, went to Meeting. Just as they left the house, Cecily and her mother came down the steps on their way to Saint Peter's. They wore beautiful new spring bonnets, and their hooped silk skirts rustled deliciously. Hannah could hear her mother's silk skirt rustle a little, too, but more softly.

Hannah looked back. Mother's dear face was framed in her black bonnet, and the folds of her snow-white fichu peeked above the black cape she wore.

"Why, she looks just as pretty as Mrs. Gibson," thought Hannah, but her own bonnet pinched her ears and was very

hot. She untied it. Just as they reached the Meeting house Becky happened to see it.

"Here, Nanny," she said, "thy bonnet is untied. Let me fix it!" She tied it tighter than ever. They all filed into the Meeting; the boys and the men on one side, the women and the girls on the other. Father, who was an elder, sat with the other elders on benches that were raised at the front and facing the congregation. Several women sat on the facing benches, too.

The Meeting was a quiet one.

The silence settled down. Hannah wondered if that was what they meant by the "weight of the Meeting."

Then a little breeze moved the branch of the sycamore that was just outside the window. It showed tiny new leaves at the tips and seemed to point like a long-fingered hand straight at Hannah.

Someone sighed gently.

Father shifted a little on the "facing" bench.

Sarah Whitall gently cleared her throat.

Isaac Stokes crossed one knee slowly over the other.

It was still again.

Hannah thought of Cecily's sash. She wished she knew how to tell Mother about it. Then someone in the back of the room got up to speak. Hannah knew it was a woman because she heard the faint rustling of her full skirts as she stood up.

The woman began.

At first Hannah didn't listen. She watched a robin hopping in the sycamore tree. She looked up into the youth's gallery and saw Richard Fox looking across toward the young women's gallery where Becky sat with Alice. She made mouths at Sally across Mother's lap.

The woman went on talking.

Suddenly all the small noises quieted, and there was not a sound through the room except the voice of the woman speaking.

Her words seemed to carry across the Meeting as if each one had wings.

Hannah listened. "And I feel a concern," the woman said, "for one in this meeting who has a secret sin."

Hannah's mind flew to the bedding chest in the attic. She saw the borrowed sash with its greasy smear.

"Be sure that sin will find thee out," the woman was saying. "Perhaps that sin is a secret vanity: vanity that has allowed the love of the things of this world to crowd out the things of the spirit." Hannah felt a wave of heat go over her. Her hands grew damp, and she drew off her mitts. Her bonnet became unbearable. She untied it. How could the woman know about the sash? she thought. How could anybody know?

Hannah looked at Father up on the facing bench. He was holding his hand over his eyes.

She looked at Mother sitting in quiet meditation.

No one was looking at her. No one was paying her the slightest attention, not even the Friend who was speaking.

Maybe they didn't *really* know anything about the sash! Her face cooled, and the dampness dried on her hands. She swallowed and moistened her lips.

Never again would she borrow anything! Never again would she let Old Spotty talk her into trouble if she could only get out of it this time! The woman stopped speaking and sat down.

After a few moments of silence Father leaned over to shake hands with Isaac Stokes. The Meeting was over.

All day long, while Father was reading aloud, while Norah was serving dinner, and even when Cousin Sophie and Uncle Jerry came to call, Hannah wondered what she could do about the sash.

When Father gave the children their weekly allowance the next morning Hannah decided:

"That is what I must do! I must save every week till I have enough to buy a new sash for Cecily."

Sally wondered why Hannah didn't want cinnamon buns from the woman who sold them at recess.

"Is thee sick, Nanny?" she asked. Hannah shook her head and tried not to smell the sugary cinnamon. When the girls were given permission to go to the shop nearby for cream puffs Hannah stayed to help Teacher Elizabeth clean the boards. They all came back looking well fed, and Sally had powdered sugar on her cheek.

"Thee doesn't know what thee's missed!" she said. "Ummm! They were good." Hannah stamped her foot.

"Why, Nanny, what's the matter with thee?" Sally asked, surprised. But Hannah pursed her mouth and wouldn't answer.

Every day after school, for the next two weeks, the girls had to help with preparations for Yearly Meeting. Toward the last there was a great moving about of furniture. Extra beds were put up; one in the big girls' room and one in John and Charlie's room. The trundle bed was brought from the attic, and when Hannah saw her mother going up there she knew the sash would be found! It was too late to do anything about it. Mother opened the bedding chest to get a quilt. Hannah was on the stairs and didn't know whether to go up or down! When Mother lifted the quilt there was a flash of pink and out fell the sash!

"What is this?" asked Mother, picking it up. She looked straight at Hannah.

"Hannah, dear!" she said, "does *thee* know anything about this?"

Hannah hung her head.

"Come up here, child. *Does* thee know about it? It looks like one that Cecily wore last summer. But what is this great smear on it? It smells like the pomade that Alice uses to keep her hands smooth. Is it? Tell me!" Mother put her arm gently around Hannah.

"Is it Old Spotty again, Hannah?" Hannah nodded her head up and down. She was too ashamed to speak.

"Thee knows, dear, thy father wants thee to be happy, but he wants thee to learn that 'things' will never make thee happy. Has this sash made thee happy?"

Hannah thought nothing in the world had ever made her more *un*happy!

"Now thee must get Cecily a new sash. We will get it right away, then thee must pay for it by going without thy allowance." Hannah was so relieved to be rid of her secret vanity she threw her arms around Mother's neck and nearly smothered her.

"Yes, Mother," she said, "I will. And wait!" She ran down to the third floor and was back upstairs again in a jiffy.

"Here's the allowance for this and last week. I haven't spent a penny! But it was hard not to." Hannah felt so free and light she wanted to skip, but she helped make the beds for the company instead.

When Seventh Day came the bustle in the house was furious. First of all, after early breakfast, Hannah was allowed to go with Gammy Welsh to the market on Dock Street. Oysters must be bought, *fresh* oysters, to be pickled. The Friends from Horsham thought pickled oysters a great delicacy. Then a large fish for baking. Shad was in season, so Gammy got that and smoked fish. Along the wet pavement were large boxes of all kinds of fish: great halibut, tiny smelts, large pink salmon, and blue mackerel. There were green lobsters moving slow feelers and bubbling a little and greenish-blue clawed crabs in baskets.

"Now," said Gammy Welsh, "we must go to the spice shop."

The spice shop was fascinating. It smelled of black pepper, of seed, of coffee, and of tea. The black peppercorns, the caraway seed, and the sesame seed were in glass bottles. There were jars, too, of bay leaves, nutmegs, and stick cinnamon. Hannah thought of the cinnamon buns she would miss with no money to spend. The coffee and tea were kept in large tin canisters decorated with pictures of China and Java.

There were pictures on the walls, too, showing clipper ships being loaded with spices in foreign ports. Hannah loved it!

Gammy's large basket was so full she could hardly get the packages in it, so the man said:

"Tell you what I'll do! Here's a basket that dry ginger root

comes in from China. It's empty. I'll put the things in that, and the young lady can carry it!"

"I love baskets!" said Hannah. "And I can use this for sewing! Thank thee!"

The packages fitted in nicely. Gammy and Hannah started for home.

"Now," said Gammy when they reached the kitchen and were putting away their things, "there are the rest of the pies to make! Does thee want to fix raisins again?"

"Of course!" said Hannah.

"Of course!" said Sally, laughing as she came into the kitchen. "Mother said thee would need me too." The girls brought chairs so that they could work near Gammy while she made piecrust.

"Now tell us how thee makes piecrust, Gammy Welsh! Tell us as thee goes," said Hannah.

"Well," said Gammy as she measured flour into a bowl, "thee takes a third as much lard as thee has flour; good *leaf* lard, thee knows! Rub it lightly together. *Lightly*, remember! My mother used to say, 'It takes the hand of a duchess to make good piecrust.' Then thee takes a small quantity of water—very cold water—and puts it in a little at a time. Then thee whacks it out on the board." Gammy Welsh "whacked" it out as she spoke. "Then thee rolls it gently. When it is very thin, thee covers it with dabs of butter and folds the dough over and rolls it out again. Then thee covers it again with dabs of butter and folds

58

again so thee can see the dabs through the dough. Of course thee knows that all this time thee's had salt in it!" Gammy finished rolling out the dough and put it into the pie tins, then she took a fork and made a crisscross pattern along the edge. Just as the pies were set in the hot oven they all heard a commotion in the hall. The company was beginning to arrive!

"Umbrellas to mend!
Umbrellas to mend!
Umbrellas! Umbrellas!
Umbrellas to mend!"

HANNAH was on her way to get the sheets from the highboy in the second-floor hall. She stopped a moment to listen to the

umbrella man, then she heard Father come up the marble steps and into the vestibule. She ran to meet him.

"We shall need all our umbrellas by the looks!" said Father, coming in just as Hannah started down the stairs. "As usual, Quaker Week will be rainy, I suppose!" He laughed and put away his beaver in the hatbox. "Have our friends arrived? I think I hear voices."

"Yes, Father," said Hannah, skipping quickly down the last few steps. She put her finger to her lips and whispered, "Sshh!

All of them! They are up in the sitting room, and we have had to put up more cots and move the washstands out into the halls and everything. Sshh! Isn't it fun?"

Hannah chuckled, and Father joined in. They went upstairs. Father turned into the sitting room to greet the company, and Hannah ran up to the third floor. She could hear Father greeting the Rhoads family and saying how glad he was that they could come after all and Margaret Rhoads saying, "I hope it won't put thee out! After I wrote saying we couldn't come Nancy seemed to improve a great deal, and we felt a concern to come. Now I am afraid thee's got a houseful!"

"Nothing we like better!" said Father. Sally was helping Mother set up another cot in the boys' room, where Mother had decided to put William and Margaret Rhoads and Tom. John and Charlie would just have to sleep in the extra beds in Father and Mother's room; one in the trundle bed and one in a cot. Nancy Rhoads would sleep on a cot in Hannah and Sally's room, and John and Mary Rhoads would sleep on a cot in Hannah and Sally's room, and John and Mary Evans in the guest room. Hannah carried the sweet-smelling sheets to Mother, but she hadn't reached the door of the bedroom before she heard the jangle of the bell, and Norah ushered in someone else! Mother had heard it too. She came out into the hall and looked down the stairwell to see who it could be.

"Hannah dear," she said, "go like a good girl and help Sally finish the bed." Then she went down. Hannah couldn't help waiting a moment to listen. She heard mother say:

"Why, Sarah Griscom! How glad I am to see thee! I thought thee was far to the south, preaching! Come into the parlor. Thee looks tired out!" Hannah went running to tell Sally that *more* company had arrived!

"*More* company!" said Sally in a whisper, with her arms full of the boys' clothes that she was moving out of the closet to make room. "What shall we *do?*"

The girls finished making the bed and looked to see that all was in order. They heard the big girls laughing and talking on their way down to supper, then heard Mother come up to call the guests in the upstairs sitting room.

"You all know Sarah Griscom!" she said. "She is to be with us too."

What a supper table! There were seventeen to sit down! Gammy Welsh and Norah had lengthened the table and found room for everybody.

The children kept their fun quiet because the grown-ups were all talking at once.

Sarah Griscom had much to tell of the meetings she had attended in the South. Once when they were speaking of the escaping slaves everyone lowered his voice. They had no fear of the children or of the servants, but as Father said, "The very walls have ears. One never knows who might be listening." And even Hannah knew that if one were discovered assisting a slave to escape it might mean great danger. It was very solemn.

While they were eating another guest arrived! It was Joshua Haines, who had come that time during the blizzard. Joshua Haines brought more news, and the talk became lively again.

After supper Mother called Hannah to her. They stepped into the pantry.

"Hannah dear, thee will have to have a bed in the bedding chest! I've thought and thought, and there is nothing else to do. Thee will have to be the one, because thee's the smallest. Joshua Haines will have to sleep on the sofa in the back parlor. It will probably be for only one night anyway. Now come and we shall see how it can be arranged." Hannah followed Mother upstairs.

When it was time for bed, Gammy Welsh brought the small whale-oil lamp to help Hannah get settled in her new sleeping place.

Mother had fluffed up the double feather tick and had helped Hannah fold a smooth clean sheet to fit the chest, then had put a cover on a sofa pillow that was just the right size. Gammy tucked her in and left the attic door open so that the light from the lamp on the stand shone through.

"What fun!" thought Hannah. "But I miss Sally. We can't play shopping tonight."

Rain drummed hard on the roof. It was warm and comfortable on the double feather tick. Hannah went to sleep.

Norah called Hannah in the morning as she came up to put away her bonnet and shawl. She and Mary Sullivan went to early church and were back in time to get breakfast. Hannah was surprised to find herself in the attic, then she remembered and, taking her clothes, went down to the third-floor room to dress with Sally. The room was full of girls! There was Sally, of course, and Nancy, and Elizabeth Rhoads, who had given up her cot in Becky and Alice's room to Sarah Griscom. There was

such a chattering that it sounded to Hannah like the sparrows in the garden.

Elizabeth was running the comb through her long hair.

"Why," thought Hannah, "it reaches to her knees almost! How I wish I had long hair like that, only black." She watched as Elizabeth pinned it in smooth coils and then put on her fine cap. Elizabeth went downstairs, and Sally followed.

"Nanny, thee better get thy hair combed too," she said. "Thee knows our mother said to be quick, because there are so many to get ready this First Day." She went on down the stairs. Hannah thought she had combed her hair, but she smoothed it again and followed the others. Everyone on the second floor seemed to have gone down too. As Hannah passed the highboy she thought of Elizabeth's long hair. She stopped and listened. There wasn't a sound on the second floor! She reached into the drawer and lifted out Mother's silk shawl. She doubled it cornerwise, then put it over her head and let it hang down her back.

"Oh," she thought, "*this* must be the way it feels to have long hair!" The shawl trailed down the steps after her as she went softly down to see what it looked like again. She went into the parlor, trailing the shawl, and there right by the window was Gammy Welsh!

Gammy heard and said, still looking out of the window, "I

guess it will rain all day. Thee'll have to wear the cover for thy bonnet." Then she turned and saw the shawl. "Thee, Hannah"— she began, but Hannah waited for no more. She flew up the stairs and put the shawl in its drawer.

Gammy had gone out of the parlor when Hannah came down, and there was so much talk going on at the table that only Mother and Sally noticed when she sat down.

"Thee's late!" said Mother. "Thee's missed the silence. What kept thee?"

Before Hannah could think up a good answer Father spoke to Mother from the other end of the table: "Joshua Haines thinks he can't come back for dinner, Martha. Can't thee urge him?" he said. Friend Haines leaned forward to say something too. As he did so, his cuff sleeve knocked over the saltcellar

standing near his plate, and a shower of salt spread over the cloth. He looked embarrassed.

"Now," he said, "I've done it again! What *was* it I did the last time I was here? *Something!*"

"Ate biscuits," said Hannah before she stopped to think. Mother looked at her.

"Why, *Hannah!*" she began, but Joshua Haines and everybody else laughed so hard that Mother didn't say any more.

After breakfast there was much bustling about to get things in order. The little girls were sent up to make beds and tidy the rooms.

"Don't forget your rainy-day bonnet covers!" called Mother as they went up.

When meeting was over the men stood waiting for their wives, and some of the young men for the young women they liked best. Richard Fox walked with Becky, Alice and Nancy were together and the Evans girls walked with Sally and Hannah under Father's big whalebone umbrella.

Mother invited Richard Fox to stay, and the table was nearly filled again. Hannah looked around the table. "Mary Evans' dress is *almost* blue!" she thought. "Elizabeth's is dark red, and Nancy's is *really* blue! Maybe now that Father has seen them he will let me have a blue dress when I go to the big school next year." Norah handed her the pickled oysters, and she was so interested in thinking of the possible blue dress that she almost took some. Hannah didn't like pickled oysters, but how the company from the country enjoyed them!

While the grown-ups sat at the table the boys and girls were excused. It was still raining, so they had to find ways to keep quiet. Hannah stood at the front window looking out at the rain.

She saw Cecily leave the house with her mother, her skirts flirting this way and that under the big umbrella, her pantalettes showing white at every step. How Hannah wished *she* had a hoop skirt and pantalettes like Cecily!

She thought of Elizabeth and how neat she looked in her red dress, with the pantalettes showing beneath. How pretty they were!

The next day Father invited several other guests for dinner, and there were twenty-five people to be fed! The children had to wait. It seemed to Hannah as if the grown-ups would never be through. The good odors came out from the dining room, but they didn't fill the empty place in Hannah's middle. She stamped her foot.

"If they would only eat and get through!" she said, "it wouldn't be so bad waiting, but they talk and *talk.*"

"Hush, Hannah!" said Sally from the stairs. "Shhh! They'll hear thee!"

She went on up to play with Sophronie, and Hannah

stamped up after her. She didn't follow Sally into the sitting
room but went to the highboy to get Mother's shawl and play
lady again. She opened the wrong drawer, then, seeing something lacy, lifted it up to see what it was. It looked like a petticoat, but not the plain ones Hannah wore. It was yellowed with
age and had tucks and lace six inches deep.

"Just like Cecily's pantalettes," she thought. "This must be something old that Mother moved out of one of the bureau drawers to make room. I guess it isn't much good, it's so old." She started to the sewing room and laid it out on the cutting table. The scissors were lying close by. Hannah picked them up and said to herself:

"If I cut it just here and here and sew up the sides, I'm sure it will be all right." But as she took up the scissors she had a "stop" in her mind that maybe it was *not* all right! Then she thought, with a delicious thrill, how elegant the pantalettes would look below her dress. Snip! Snip! went the scissors through the tucks and lace.

When Hannah lifted out the pieces she had cut, a great black hole was left. It looked *dreadful!* "But," she thought, "how fashionable the pantalettes will look!" She got out a needle and thread but didn't bother with the troublesome thimble.

Big stitches didn't matter either and would go faster. Hannah sewed up the seams in no time, but when it came to putting on a band she didn't know what to do.

"I know," she thought, "I'll just pin them to my drawer body." She took some pins from the beaded pincushion and, tucking the pantalettes under her arm, ran up to the third-floor bedroom. Her dress and petticoat kept getting in the way, so she took them off. Pinning on the new finery wasn't as easy as she had thought, but it was finally done, and the petticoat and the dress were put on. A peek into Becky's mirror seemed necessary, and Hannah had to climb onto a chair to see the effect. Even then the mirror was too high for her to see much.

The pantalettes didn't look just as she expected they would, but, "They'll have to do," she said, and then went down to show Sally. Sally had left the sitting room and gone downstairs, so Hannah went down too. She heard the people coming from the dining room but went on. Something slipped! One of the pins had come out! Before Hannah could catch herself another pin dropped out, and the pantalettes slipped down and tripped her. She went rolling down the stairs and landed right at Mother's feet!

"Hannah! Hannah! What *has* thee been doing now?" asked Mother as she helped her up. The pantalettes were so tangled around Hannah's feet that Mother had to take them off before

she could move. Mother didn't say a word but looked at her with a discouraged sigh.

Fortunately the company went on into the parlor, and only Father stayed to see what had happened.

"Thee seems to be in difficulty again, Hannah!" he said. Mother motioned for him to go into the parlor, too, and took Hannah upstairs.

"Thee seems to listen to Old Spotty more than thee listens to thy mother," she said as they went up. "Now thee *knows* for thyself that pride goeth before a fall. Thee's cut up my mother's wedding petticoat too. That grieves me, but it grieves me more to see thee set so much store by worldly things. Thee knows that when thee is older thee can wear things that are not seemly for a little girl. *I* wouldn't mind if thee had pantalettes, but thy Father is an elder, and he feels that little girls should learn early not to think too much of what they wear." By this time Hannah and her Mother had reached the sitting room, and Hannah was weeping quietly.

"I didn't know the petticoat was any good," she said. Mother went on talking.

"Didn't thee have a 'stop' in thy mind? I had bought material for a blue dress for thee, and we would have made it for thy birthday, but now, thee's not ready for it. Thee must wait till

thee has learned that the color of the dress doesn't matter. That pantalettes and sashes do not matter, and thee must learn what thy bonnet stands for. Thee must learn Quaker ways." Mother patted Hannah's shoulder and told her to sit and think about it.

Hannah thought and *thought,* but couldn't quite understand what it all meant. Why she and Sally couldn't wear things the big girls wore. And what did her plain, ugly bonnet stand for? She wondered. But she was very unhappy to have made Mother sad, and when she went downstairs she hoped she could remember to do everything just as Father wished.

Then came Sixth Day morning. Norah was called home to care for her mother who had been taken ill. Sally stayed to help Gammy Welsh instead of going to meeting with the others.

After meeting Mother said to Hannah, "Before *we* go home, let us go to Eighth Street and buy the sash for Cecily. Would thee and Mary Evans like to come along?" she said to Margaret Rhoads.

Hannah thought how much fun it would be to buy the sash, even though it was not for herself.

"It must have a good body," said Mother to the saleswoman, "and be of as good quality as the one that was spoilt." She brought the sash out of her large bag and compared the two in the light. How Hannah wished that lovely new sash were for her! It would help to make her new muslin not quite so plain. Oh, why had Old Spotty whispered to her that the lace petticoat would make pantalettes like Cecily's? It still hurt to think she couldn't have the blue dress for her birthday—that she would have to wait and wait.

On Sixth Day afternoon Hannah took the soiled sash and the new one back to Cecily. It was hard to give up the lovely silk, especially when Mrs. Gibson wanted her to keep it.

One of Cecily's bonnets lay on the bed.

"Oh!" exclaimed Hannah. "How pretty it is!"

"Try it on!" said Cecily. She whisked it off the bed and onto Hannah's head. Hannah turned to look in the mirror to see how it looked. Before she knew it, Cecily was unbuttoning her dress and helping her into another. A *blue* one to match the ribbons on the bonnet!

Just then Mrs. Gibson called from the other room, "Will you girls go to the Rectory for me to take a message? It really should go immediately. I have the note here, Cecily."

Cecily hurried back with the note. "Oh, Hannah-Nanny," she said, "you look so pretty in my bonnet. Don't change it. Come on, Mamma says this report should be there, and it is getting late." The clothes didn't seem strange to Cecily, because she wore them all the time. Hannah had a "stop" in her mind that perhaps she shouldn't go without putting on her own bonnet and dress, but the dress made her eyes so blue and the bonnet felt so much cooler and was so much prettier than her own that she went along with Cecily as she was.

Hannah felt very worldly as she flounced along down Pine Street, and the farther they got away from home the more she thought it was all right. But as they came out of the Rectory, she saw a group of Friends down the block. And suddenly the fun was gone. What if they had seen her?—Hannah, whose father was an elder!

The girls went up Spruce Street on their way home. And then just as they turned the corner at Twelfth, Father came toward them with two of the other elders. Hannah wished the earth would open and swallow her. Father looked at her sternly.

"Thee, Hannah!" he said, "get thee into the house and into thy proper clothes."

"Oh!" she thought, "I've let Old Spotty get me into trouble again. Now what will happen?" She hurried to get into the house with Cecily and into her own clothes.

The company was leaving when she got home, so Father didn't scold her, but he still looked very stern. And for Hannah all the joy of Quaker Week was gone.

"Peaches, soft ripe peaches!
Delaware peaches! Peaches, peaches!"
THROUGH the garden gate Hannah could see the woman with
a tray on her head as she passed. Gammy Welsh wouldn't need

to buy any peaches, because there was a tree loaded with them right in the garden. Hannah sighed as she put her needle in and out of the calico pieces. She was all alone in the grape arbor sewing pieces for a quilt. Sally was in the country visiting the Evans family, and Cecily was with her family at the seashore.

Before school had closed a letter had come from Mary Evans saying: "We should like to have the younger girls for a visit as soon as school is over. I know that the boys are to go to the Rhoads' and Rebecca wrote that she and Alice are to go to Cape May—"

But Father had said, "I'm afraid thee's not old enough to go, Hannah. Thee doesn't seem to be able to remember thee's a Friend." It was very hard for Hannah to let Sally go without her but she knew Father was thinking of that awful day of Quaker Week when he said she wasn't old enough to go.

Mother had said, "Hannah dear, we will try to help thee this summer to understand what it means to be a Friend. And since Norah has to stay at home, I really need thy help." So Hannah had done a good deal of running up and down stairs, doing errands and helping with dish washing and bed making. She had learned to use her thimble too, but she still hated her plain hot bonnet.

On First Day, when they had come from Meeting, Hannah had stayed on in the garden. The warm air drew out the fra-

grance of the mignonette and wallflower and the spicy odors from Mother's herb garden. The bleeding hearts hung like jewels from the stem, and Hannah thought, "What a lovely bracelet they would make!" So she fastened them around her wrist. Then, as she loosened her bonnet, she thought, "Why wouldn't these flowers look pretty inside my bonnet?" Off came the bonnet as Hannah ran into the house to find pins. Pinks and forget-me-nots looked pretty together, and two buds from the rose garden with their glossy leaves just filled in the frame of the bonnet. Hannah put it on, then leaned to the shed window to peer in just as Mother's quiet voice said from the doorway:

"Dinner is ready, Hannah dear. Come wash thy hands."

Hannah snatched off her bonnet, but not before Mother had seen the flowery trimming.

"What's thee up to now, child?" She took the bonnet from Hannah's hand. The flowers had already begun to wilt, and where they had been pinned the silk was stained and crumpled.

"I see thee still doesn't understand that our plain bonnets stand for something. And see how thee has spoiled this costly silk! But thee has to wear it just the same. After dinner thee must sit out here quietly and think about it." Mother threw the wilted flowers away.

After dinner Hannah had sat, as Mother said, and tried to understand, but as she looked up through the grape leaves to the blue sky she was fascinated by the shapes of clouds that passed slowly by. She heard someone singing in the next street and was filled with longing to sing too. Two ladies in full hoop skirts and bright bonnets went by. They were carrying parasols with lace ruffles on the edges, and their ribbons floated airily as they walked.

"Why," Hannah wondered, "why are they different from us? Why is it all right for them to dress that way when we can't?" And once again she asked herself as she had so many times that summer, "Will I ever be like Mother and not care about pretty bonnets?"

It had been a hot and long summer for Hannah, even though Mother kept her busy through most of the mornings. The afternoons were especially lonely. The shutters were bowed to keep out the heat, and Mother always took a rest. Hannah was supposed to rest too, but the cries of the street vendors, the bell of the scissor grinder, the cry of the ragman, who seemed to say "Rags alarn," the "Clop! Clop!" of horses' feet on the cobbles, and the grating of the iron-rimmed wheels all came through the heated air. Hannah couldn't sleep.

One day Mother had said, "Why not make a quilt?" And though it wasn't much fun to sew without Sally, Hannah did like the bright calico pieces. Mother had helped her cut the first blocks, then said, "Thee must cut thy own."

"But," said Hannah, "I don't like to cut. I want to get at it and sew them together so I can see how it will look. See! I can cut several pieces together!"

"I am afraid they will slip and not be cut true and straight," said Mother.

"Oh, yes," said Hannah. "I will hold it tight and be careful. It will be much quicker."

"Yes, dear, when I was nine I thought I knew better than my mother too. Well, thee must try and see." Hannah folded the bits of cloth and put several together, then she put the pattern on and cut around it.

"Now," she said, "there will be four pieces ready to sew instead of one." She took the pattern off and separated the little pieces of calico. Mother was watching and saw Hannah's pleased look go. One piece hadn't quite come to the edge of the pattern. One had been wrinkled and had to be cut over; one had been folded instead of flat. The only piece that came out right was the one on top!

"Thee sees, Hannah, in anything we like to do there is always some part that takes time and isn't so pleasant. It is always so."

"Yes, Mother, thee's right," said Hannah. She cut the other pieces one by one.

Finally she had enough pieces cut to begin on the sewing, and Mother showed her how to put them together with tiny stitches. She sewed till suppertime. She sewed all the next day. Then it was time to cut again. When Hannah sighed because she didn't like that part Mother said, "If thee works faithfully every day, you might get the quilt done for Becky's wedding."

"Becky's wedding!" exclaimed Hannah. "To Richard?"

"To Richard as ever was!" Mother answered, smiling. Then Hannah began cutting pieces furiously. Gammy Welsh said to her:

"If thee gets that quilt done in time for Becky's wedding, I'll give thee a dinner party and serve it on solid gold plates." She chuckled as she went on about her work.

"Solid gold plates!" echoed Hannah. She went to work harder than ever.

Hannah worked all the sultry August day. In the late afternoon Mother called her in. "Thee, Hannah dear, will have to go with this basket of things for Norah," she said. "Thee knows it isn't so very far, and I'm sure she needs these things I promised her. There is some old linen, and thee can take this fresh butter from market and some of the peaches. There is a piece of Mary's loaf cake too. Thee'll have to put thy straw bonnet on. The sun is still hot."

Hannah got her bonnet. She hated it worse than ever now that the silk lining was stained. She still remembered how pretty the flowers had looked—almost as pretty as in Cecily's bonnet.

"Now," said Mother, "mind how thee goes and don't linger on the way. Be sure to ask Norah how her mother fares and if there is anything else we can do for her." Mother tied Hannah's bonnet and made her put on her mitts. "So thee'll look like a little lady," she said.

Hannah went down Twelfth Street and around the corner. The street seemed very empty, and little shimmering waves of heat rose from the bricks and cobbles. Some of the vestibules stood invitingly open. Some had flowers standing in large jars, the white marble gleaming and cool. Many of the houses were closed for the summer. The people were at the seashore or in the country.

As Hannah passed one such house she said to herself, "Yes, these people must be away too, because the steps are dusty, there are papers on the pavement, and the poplar leaves are just where they fell." She saw the solid wooden gate between it and the next house. Slowly it opened, and the face of a Negro woman looked out.

"Missy!" she said very low. "Oh, missy!" Hannah was frightened, but the woman looked so thin and worn she felt she must at least listen to her. "Missy, *please* help me!" the woman said again. "Ise got a sick chile heah an' we ain't got no water and no food. *Please,* Missy, get yo' mammy or yo' pappy an' help me."

Just then Hannah saw a man coming up the street. She slipped into the alleyway where the woman was. There on the brick pavement lay a child who looked at Hannah with great brown eyes. He didn't say anything when the woman knelt beside him. There was only a ragged old coat between him and the bricks.

"This li'l lady is gwine he'p me," she said to him. "Don' yo' fret, chile, Mammy's here an' we's gwine git to yo' pappy yit!" Then she turned to Hannah, who had stood wondering what to do. She spoke scarcely above a whisper. "We was on our way to de No'th where dis chile's pappy is free! Bless de Lawd! But de chile took sick, and I tried to make him betta but I didn't have no way to take keer of him."

They heard the man passing and waited till his footsteps were far off. Hannah opened her basket and took out the loaf cake.

"Take this," she said, "and I'll go tell Mother. I promise thee I won't be long!"

Hannah opened the gate and hurried back up to Twelfth Street then around the corner and home.

"Mother!" she called, "Gammy Welsh!" as she ran up the steps and knocked for someone to open the door. But it was Father who opened the door. Hannah told him about the Negro woman and the child. Even as he was listening he was putting on his big straw hat, and as Hannah finished he called to Mother.

When she had heard the pitiful story she said, "The woman will have to come here until she is able to go on. We can put her upstairs in the little back room." She called Gammy to help her. They put more food into the basket and found a bottle for water.

"We'll keep supper hot, but hurry back," she said, "so we can arrange things."

"I will be back in a few moments, Martha." Then, taking Hannah's hand, Father said, "Come, child, show me." They went as fast as Hannah could walk. She was still carrying her basket and was so warm from hurrying she started to untie her bonnet, then thought better of it as she remembered what Mother had said about looking like a lady.

The street was still empty, though there were two men passing over Tenth Street.

"It is there," said Hannah. "There, between the two empty houses." They slipped in the high gate. At first it was too dark to see, and the woman was so startled she couldn't speak. Then she recognized Hannah.

"It's you, li'l missy. Thank yo' fo de food. See! My chile is betta already! But he's so thi'sty. Dey's water in de ga'den here but I dassen't git it fo' night. We's been here fo' two days!" The poor woman was ready to drop with weariness and hunger, but she smiled at Hannah.

"Poor soul, poor soul," said Father, leaning over to look at the little boy. "Here's water for thee, and after dark I'll contrive some way to come for thee. Thee knows the danger there is. But I'll find a way. Be patient a little longer. We shall find thee a bed for tonight somehow." They left the woman and went back to see what could be done.

Darkness seemed long in coming that night. Hannah couldn't help thinking of the poor slave woman and the little boy. Finally it was dark enough for Father to think it safe to go for her. Mother put her oldest bonnet and shawl into the basket and a little old roundabout that had been John's for the little boy.

"What shall we do about hiding the little boy's face?" she asked.

"He's so small," said Father, "I think if thee's got another shawl, I could wrap him, head and all, and carry him. We can get through one of the back streets and come in the back way."

Hannah was watching when the dark figures came in the back gate and up the garden walk. The Negro woman had hold of Father's arm and her head was bent down. The little boy was in Father's arms, his head hidden by a plaid shawl of Gammy's. They were safe!

Mary Sullivan had set out food for the two, and before they had finished eating, the little boy was smiling.

The woman told how she had run away from a cruel master, how she had traveled at night, walking weary miles, sometimes finding a ride hidden in a load of hay or in a wagon carrying boxes of goods.

"I knowed if we come to Philadelphia and git to de ribber, maybe we kin find a Friend and git to Boston on a boat. De chile's pappy sen' word about it."

Then she told how she had been hidden in a farmer's wagon between sacks of vegetables. The boy had been sick and weak, and the heat was almost unbearable. The farmer had stopped at a tavern outside the city, and because it was dusk she had dared to take the child out for a breath of air and to get water from the trough at the pump she had seen around the corner of the inn. While she was gone the farmer had come out and driven off, so under cover of darkness she had walked as far as she could, carrying the boy most of the way.

Finally she couldn't carry him any longer, and he was too weak to walk. In trying to reach the river she had gotten as far as Pine Street, then, seeing the houses closed and shuttered for the summer, she had hidden between them in the covered alleyway. There Hannah had found her.

The woman and boy were both too weak and sick to go on

their way for a few days, so Mother and Hannah took care of them in the little back room till Father could arrange some way for them to go on. Hannah lost all interest in the quilt making and said, "I couldn't get it done for Becky's wedding anyway."

Gammy laughed as she picked up Hannah's sewing basket and put it away. "I knew I was perfectly safe in promising solid gold plates for that dinner," she said. "I was a little girl once myself."

Hannah went up and down stairs many times a day to take food and water to the sick woman. Mother and Gammy bathed her and made her comfortable. Father came home with the news that he had arranged a passage for her with the captain of a boat who was a Friend. She and the boy were to be taken after nightfall to the wharf, where the boat was being loaded with goods for Boston. The woman's husband was working there in a shipyard.

It all had to be done with the greatest secrecy, for those who helped escaping slaves were hated even by some people who didn't keep them. If the woman was found by anyone searching for escaping slaves, she would be punished and sent back to her owner or perhaps killed.

Father hired a carriage to take the woman to the wharf. Mother dressed her in one of her dark dresses and put the bonnet on her again. She found more of the boys' old clothes and altered them to fit the little black boy. And finally she dusted their faces with flour so they would not look so black in case anyone should see them passing.

When it was time to go Mother went along in the carriage and took Hannah to help hide the little boy.

They got safely to the boat, and the captain hurried them below to the cabin he had ready.

The woman was so grateful she could scarcely speak, and tears filled her eyes as she took Father's and Mother's hands. Then she turned to Hannah.

"Li'l missy," she said, "it's *you* dat he'ped me first. I knowed I could trus' *you*. I knowed you was a *Friend* 'cause of yo' Quaker bonnet." Hannah's fingers reached up to touch her bonnet. Somehow it didn't feel tight any longer. It felt light and beautiful. It was something to be proud of just as it was—without any flowers or ribbons like Cecily's. She looked up at Mother with the "inner light" shining through her eyes.

"Thee dear, Hannah!" said Mother.

MARGUERITE DE ANGELI was born in 1889 in Lapeer, Michigan. During her long, productive life she wrote twenty-eight books for young readers that won her a large and faithful audience as well as many prestigious awards. The honors she received include the Newbery medal, two Caldecott Honor Awards, the Lewis Carroll Shelf Award, and the Regina Medal. A mother, grandmother, and great-grandmother, Mrs. de Angeli found her own family a vital source of inspiration. Each of her books reflects the wisdom and personal warmth that has earned her a special place in the hearts of generations of young readers.